The Windy Day

G. Brian Karas

Simon & Schuster Books for Young Readers

SIMON & SCHUSTER BOOKS FOR YOUNG READERS

An imprint of Simon & Schuster Children's Publishing Division

1230 Avenue of the Americas New York, New York 10020

Copyright © 1998 by G. Brian Karas

SIMON & SCHUSTER BOOKS FOR YOUNG READERS

is a trademark of Simon & Schuster.

Book design by Paul Zakris

The text of this book is set in 25-point Kosmik-Bold Three.

Printed and bound in the United States of America

First Edition 10 9 8 7 6 5 4 3 2 1

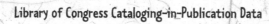

Library of Congress Cataloging-in-Publication Data

Karas, G. Brian

The windy day / by G. Brian Karas.

p.   cm.

Summary: One day the wind blows into a tidy little town,

giving a tidy little boy named Bernard a hint of how wonderful and

exciting the world is.

ISBN: 0-689-81449-6

[1. Winds—Fiction.]   I. Title

PZ7.K1276W1 1998   [E]—dc21   97-25427

For Margo and Patty

ABOUT THE ART

The artist worked on the windiest-looking paper he could find.

Bits of grass, newspapers, and flowers blow through this breezy book.

Pencils, gouache, and acrylic paints were also used.

One day a little breeze peeled off the trade winds and went its own way. It blew over smooth hills. It skipped over choppy seas. Whistling a song through the treetops, it gathered up speed and headed for a tidy town.

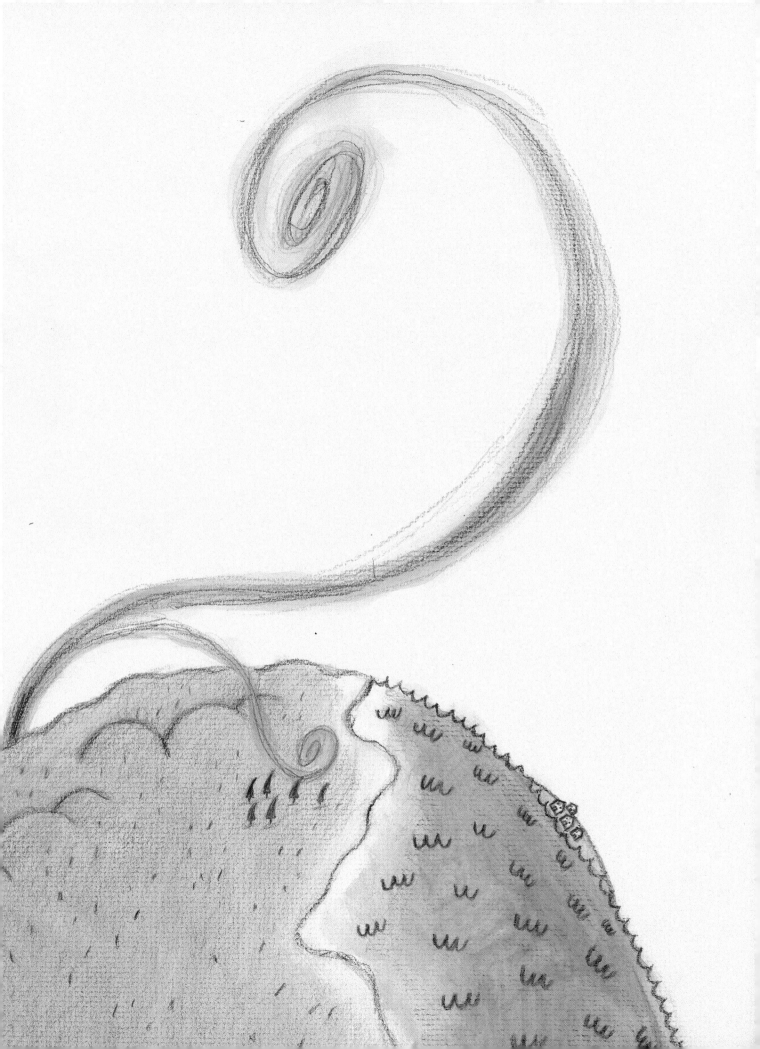

In the tidy town everyone was getting dressed,

eating breakfast,

and going about their business,

just like every day.

In a tidy house in the tidy town
a young boy was getting dressed.
Underpants, then socks, then
pants, then shirt, then shoes . . .
and always in that order.

He ate breakfast.
One bowl of crispies,
one half a banana,
one glass of milk,

and went

to school.

H-o-o-o-o-o-hummmmmmmm.

$\mathcal{B}ut$ when the wind whooshed into town,

it swept up leftover pancakes, eggs, and oatmeal, alarm clocks, dominoes, bananas, photographs, newspapers, and notepads.

It swept up house paint, geraniums, math papers, spelling tests, toothbrushes, cupcakes, and cream puffs.

Only the boy turned
and faced the wind,
and he breathed in

the breath of long-ago kings and queens.

He felt air that touched
the edge of outer space,
that traveled along
the Great Wall of China,

air that ruffled the hairs
of polar bears living at
the North Pole.

He breathed in air that blew the dust off pyramids,
brushed the hands of Big Ben, and filled Viking sails.
Air that burst from ancient volcanoes,
swayed the coconut palms over
Bluebeard's island, and tickled a dinosaur's chin.

Then just as it came,
the wind went.
The boy watched it go.
"My name is Bernard!"
he yelled.

The wind swept up his words
and made its way out
into the still afternoon,

which was not to be still for long.